HELLO KITTY®
and
♥ME♥

Best Friends

Copyright © 2014 by Sanrio Co., Ltd.
Cover and internal design © 2014 by Sourcebooks, Inc.
Cover design by Randee Ladden and Brittany Vibbert
Text by Jacqueline A. Ball
Internal design by Jason Lavicky

Published by Sourcebooks Jabberwocky, an imprint of Sourcebooks, Inc.
P.O. Box 4410, Naperville, Illinois 60567-4410
(630) 961-3900
Fax: (630) 961-2168
www.jabberwockykids.com

Library of Congress Cataloging-in-Publication data is on file with the publisher.

Source of Production: Worzalla, Stevens Point WI, USA
Date of Production: May 2014
Run Number: 5001668

Printed and bound in the United States of America.
WOZ 10 9 8 7 6 5 4 3 2 1

Hello Kitty has lots of friends. Now she has a new friend, too. Guess who?

It's YOU!

Win or lose, it doesn't matter–best friends always cheer each other on.

Best friends journey through life together.

Friends take turns going up and down.

Friends help each other swing high!

The **seasons** change, but best friends stick together.

Friends love to have fun in the sun!

They make each day a new adventure!

Friends make snowmen and have snowball fights.

When clouds bring rain, friends bring rainbows.

They laugh and play
all year long.

Best friends like to do new things together.

They explore new places. Everything looks so tiny from up here!

Wherever they go, friends make the sweetest music. Sing along!

Friends share their stories.

They draw pictures
of their favorite things.

Hello Kitty and her friends are wishing on a star.

They are wishing you will come back and play again soon!

Hello Kitty is SO HAPPY you are her new FRIEND!